Barely Remembered

by

C Faherty Brown

©2024

All Rights Reserved

ISBN: 979-8-9918408-2-8

It sits out in the country. Alone. No town nearby. No school. No church stands there. Long ago a small church did stand. It stood, as you looked at the cemetery from the road, to the far left. All of the graves to the right. The church had been small, built by the few families who wished to worship together. Built on a foundation of stone dug from their fields, logs and boards from their own trees, pews built from those same trees. Windows were small and covered with shutters, glass was added as the families could afford the expense of it.

As those families aged, their young grew into adults and many moved to more populated areas.

Long before the fire took the church it had sat unused, dying out as the local families had died out. A few returned but only to be laid to rest in a place they remembered fondly and wished had not changed.

The stones of the foundation eventually worked themselves back into the ground. Though some had also found their way into the foundations of nearby homes, barns or other foundations.

The cemetery's last known burial was in 1972. There was no name of the cemetery posted. Most folks who knew of it just called it 'the old cemetery'. Its remote location would have left it to nature to take over but for some old farmers who took turns cutting and trimming the grass. They had a respect for whoever the people were. Most of them unknown.

Though unknown to the world today those lain to rest in the old cemetery had lived.

Mercy Wheatson

1783-1813

"It's a girl!" Though not always met with joy, this announcement in the Wheatson family was cheered inside and outside of the cabin.

Mercy's Ma, Alice, had given Pa nine strong boys. They all felt happy for Ma that she would have a little girl to fuss over who might one day fuss over Ma.

The older boys had made a new cradle for the baby. In hopes it would be a girl they carved a rose above where her little head would lay.

Pa was smitten from the very start. It wasn't unusual to find him going back to the cabin, leaving the field or barn or woodpile, to go check on and pick up baby Mercy. Some of the boys would hear Pa telling Ma the only prettier girl anywhere, then Mercy, was Mercy's Ma.

Mercy's brothers loved to play with her. When she got older they would use their foraging burlap sacks, hung on their shoulders, to carry her around. Ma finally told them they would have to put her on her feet or she would never learn to walk. Every night after that the boys would make a circle around Mercy and try to get her to walk. There were no cheers louder in the country then when Mercy Wheaton took her first steps at only 9 months old.

Mercy was everyone's favorite. But she was closest in age and fondness to Isaac. Isaac was 3 years old when Mercy was born. Both had full heads of curly, dark hair. They played together and slept together once Mercy outgrew her cradle. When their little heads were together you couldn't tell who's curls were who's.

Ma and Pa insisted that all of their children pray hard, work hard and rest well. They read the Bible every night as a family. As the children were taught to read they became the nightly readers. It was a special occasion when each child became able to read out loud to the family for the first time. Ma always made a special cake, heavy and hearty, to celebrate.

The first night Mercy read the Bible to the family, brothers who had gotten married, built their own cabins, and had their own babies, all crowded into Ma and Pa's cabin when Mercy was to read out loud for the first time. She felt confident, for that is what her family gave her, as she stood at eight years old in front of them all. Pa set her up on the table and kept a hand at her back. She read "Jesus said 'let the little children come to me, and do not hinder them, for the kingdom of heavens belongs to such as these'". She had practiced for weeks, eventually memorizing it. But it was her turn to read so she held the Bible and with slow and careful words was the last of Ma and Pa's children to read the nightly bible scripture for the first time.

Everyone told her she had done wonderful. But everyone felt the sadness of it as well. Mercy didn't until the older brothers and their families had left. The cabin suddenly seemed bigger. Less lively. She looked at Ma who smiled and held Mercy's chin for a minute "well done Mercy, God is pleased."

Mercy and Isaac went to the loft to sleep. But first, as they always did before falling into the wonderful sleep of loved children, they whispered about their day.

"That was strong reading Mercy".

"Thank you Isaac. Did you think everyone was sad?"

Isaac thought quietly. "Yes. Not at your reading. It was a good reading for all the children to hear."

"Why do you think?"

Isaac, laying on his bed of deerskin, turned his head to look at her as she lay on her own deerskin bed. "We're all a-growing Mercy".

It was Mercy's turn to be thoughtful. Growing should be good. But she knew when the 'olders' left this evening it was different.

From that night on Mercy became more aware, a student of her family's lives. She noticed changes in Ma and Pa, how they looked or acted. She paid closer attention to her brothers, and as they married, she watched their wives. She watched behaviors, actions, and listened to words. She loved her family dearly and thought them the salt of the earth. She learned from them how to be loyal, hard working, dependent and independent. It wasn't a bad thing to need one another.

When Isaac turned seventeen he asked Pa to help him build his own cabin. Isaac wanted to stay close but a little nearer the river. The brothers and wives all helped and in no time they had a three room cabin with a loft. Everyone knew what was coming. Isaac had fallen for the sister of one of the brother's wives. They married shortly after the cabin was done. Isaac and Abigail were hardworking and loving. They reminded everyone of Ma and Pa. They hoped on having as many children as Ma and Pa. At first when it didn't happen they tried all of the trusted remedies. Nothing happened. As the years went on everyone quietly avoided talking about it. As babies were born to others no one rejoiced more then Issac and Abigail.

Abigail and Mercy became very close. Abigail often helping Mercy as Ma grew tired, quicker.

Like Isaac Mercy fell in love with a brother's wife's sibling. His name, Amos, and he was from the same family as Abigail. Amos was quiet and hard working. He was intrigued by everything. He and Mercy loved to discover and create. They built their own furniture, like most folks did, but did so in creative ways. They carved trees and flowers into everything they made. They made miniature boats for the children to float on the river.

When they had decided to marry Ma and Pa offered them the large cabin if they would all help Ma and Pa build a smaller cabin. The smaller cabin was built across the yard from Mercy and Amos.

Mercy was almost relieved when she did not immediately become pregnant. Her solidarity with Isaac and Abigail put her of the mind that it would be too painful to have a child to love and they have none. Amos expressed some concern initially about no children being born to them. But he also recognized they were surrounded by children everywhere. It was as if all of the children belonged to them in some way. Seldom, if ever, did a day go past when a niece, nephew, or several, weren't in and about the house all day long. And often through the nights.

Amos, Mercy, Abigail and Isaac felt no less important to the family. They became confidants to children and siblings alike. They were the first sought out to share joys and sorrows. Ma and Pa were still working hard but grateful to be surrounded by their children and families, with always willing hands to make their work less difficult.

Then, long past any expectation of it, Mercy was pregnant. She was almost thirty years old. She was many months along before she knew. Ma and Pa were happiest of all.

Mercy and Abigail had grown so close it was Abigail who Mercy confided joys and fears to.

One hot summer night, with sweat plastering the hair to their necks, they sat at the river with their feet cooling off in the water. They sat upon logs that had been placed years ago on top of stones, for just this purpose. Or to fish from.

"Abigail I have something to ask of you."

"Of course Mercy. Just ask."

Mercy was sure of what she was going to ask and how to say it but knew Abigail would have difficulty hearing it. "I want you to raise this baby".

Abigail did indeed have a difficult time hearing this. "What? You must be mad Mercy. You know I'm here to help. Of course." Mercy had it all worked out in her head to tell Abigail she knew, without knowing why she knew, that she would not be here to raise this baby. She also knew it would be a boy. She changed her mind when Abigail became upset and instead said "if anything were ever to happen to me promise me you and Isaac will raise this baby." She did not tell Abigail that she had already discussed this with Amos. Amos did not like to hear her talk like this but he did promise her. He did not admit it to Mercy but he didn't know if he could raise a child on his own. And he didn't know what he would do without Mercy.

Abigail reached out and took Mercy's chin in her hand, much like Ma had done years ago. "I promise". That was all Mercy needed. She did not bring the subject up again. She knew she could count on Abigail. Abigail thought many parents must have this concern. She wanted to give Mercy some ease of mind. But she didn't want to think about it.

The day came. Cool. Beautiful. It was a hard labor. Ma, Abigail and all of the sisters-in-law were there. All of the men are in Ma and Pa's cabin. There wasn't much room for moving about. Amos paced, mostly outside. The brothers would get antsy and tired of sitting. A lot of wood got chopped and the animals had extra hands tending to them.

Mercy gave birth to a fat baby boy more than 24 hours after labor started. Another cool morning. She named him Matthew after Matthew of the Bible. The first family bible reading she did so many years ago was from Matthew.

Mercy spent the day in bed with all of her female family doting on her and Matthew. Matthew lay with her, content to be with his mother. Mercy could not get enough of his softer then clouds skin. His beautiful aroma. Everything was perfect.

Until the next morning when Abigail went in to get Matthew and let Abigail rest. Amos had slept on quilts in the main room to let Mercy rest.

Abigail paused as she stepped in the room—knowing something was not right. The baby lay making little baby noises. Mercy had her arm around him, her other arm lay across herself with her hand on the baby. Her face at rest. Abigail started to cry. "Amos! Amos! Amos!" Amos, not having slept well fumbled getting up and to Abigail. He rushed past her and stopped abruptly inside the room. He paused only for a second. He stepped to the bed and scooped up his son handing him to Abigail.

Amos pulled Mercy to his chest, rocking back and forth. Abigail ran to get Ma and Pa. There were grandchildren there as well. She dispatched the children to gather the family. Ma and Pa went to Mercy.

They all went to Mercy.

Those who could see never forgot the sight of Amos rocking Mercy, or Ma and Pa who suddenly seemed old.

Amos called to Abigail who handed him Matthew. Amos held his complete family one last time. He placed Matthew on his chest with one hand and held Mercy to his chest with the other. He cried out "pray for her!" And they did. They all did.

Amos handed the baby to Abigail and told her to "take him home".

Amos left the room so the women could tend to Mercy. He insisted on helping Isaac and the brothers make the coffin. It did not take long for the tight knit family and community to prepare. An outfit was made for Mercy. She was laid out in the bed where she had birthed her son. The next day she was wrapped in linen and placed in the wooden box. The brothers carried Mercy to the graveyard. The family and friends trailed behind. Abigail carried Matthew.

When they returned home Abigail and Isaac took Matthew to Amos. Amos held the child and sobbed. His rough worked fingers softly outlining the child's face.

"Abigail. Mercy wanted you to be his mother. She knew. She knew she would not be here". He lowered his head. "How did she know?!" He raised pleading eyes to both Abigail and Isaac. Isaac placed his hand upon Amos' shoulder. No one could answer that. Neither of them tried to.

Amos stood and put Matthew in Abigail's arms. "You cannot be his mother without Isaac as his father". Abigail and Isaac looked at each other. They looked at Amos, not certain of how to react. "You must, for him."
Amos stayed for awhile in the cabin he had shared with Mercy. Then one morning, he was

gone. Isaac and Abigail raised Matthew as their own. The first time Amos returned he was welcomed with love and warmth. His cabin remained just as he had left it. And that's how it went. He would show up and stay for a day or a month. He would disappear for a year, or three. There was no prediction to it.

Matthew grew in love.

Everyone missed Mercy.

Charlie Mack

1831-1921

"I'm Charlie Mack, not Charles". The clerk wanted his full name, no nickname. "Charlie Mack it is then". "That is my name" Charlie replied to the indifferent clerk. It didn't take much more than that and he was in the army.

Charlie didn't tell his family he was leaving until the morning he left to join. They weren't surprised. He followed what was going on in the world. He believed it was the right thing to do. He took his oath as a Union Soldier that very day.

Charlie wasn't a big talker but was a do-er. By the end of the war he had seen more battles then he could have imagined man creating. He never spoke of his time in battle but he carried it with him always.

After he returned home no one could entice or aggravate Charlie into an argument. He would tell anyone who disagreed with him "I won't argue with ye but I'll talk with ye about it like men ought to do."

Charlie worked in the lumber mill. He worked hard, for himself and the company. One day he sat on the bench outside to catch a breeze and cool off while he ate his bread and cheese. Across the way, coming out of the General Store, was the prettiest girl he had ever seen.

For weeks he sat at the bench for his lunch watching for her. He learned quick enough that she was a creature of habit. Every Wednesday while he ate his lunch she came out of the General Store carrying small packages. On the fourth Wednesday he was standing in the dirt, below the wooden walkway in front of the stores as she came out.

"Ma'am". She stopped and smiled at him. "My name is Charlie Mack. I work at the mill." He looked over his shoulder to look at the mill as he said it. "I've seen you a few times and I wanted to say hello".

"Hello Charlie Mack. My name is Clara, Clara Hoy."

They married six months later.
Charlie and Clara started having children. Charlie was 42 when he married. Clara was 28 and already had a child, a boy named Henry. Charlie was good to Henry. Like all the sons that followed, Charlie taught him the fundamentals of being a man, a good person. With their daughters he felt Clara had the upper hand on being a good woman, but he still helped with the good person characteristics. Charlie and Clara made home a pleasant and faithful home.

Charlie enjoyed Henry's company. They fished and hunted together. Henry helped Charlie when he built the new little family a small house just outside of town. As the family grew so did the house. They built a comfortable outhouse, a shop, and were lucky enough to have a spring so they built a solid stone spring house.

Charlie and Henry were the first to show up when neighbors needed help. They helped build the new school house when the old one nearly fell over in a storm. They helped build the church when the community grew enough to not fit in the school house for services.

All the while they worked together they learned about one another. And they liked and respected one another. When Clara gave birth to the first son after two girls he held the small child and said to Henry "I hope this child grows with the shine of your character". Charlie didn't say much but when he did, it mattered.

Charlie still never spoke of the war. His children all knew about the war and that their father had fought as a soldier. It wasn't until a family of color came to town that Charlie's feelings were expressed. The family was worn out and worn through. The community was talking about them. But no one offered them help. No one offered comfort. When Charlie heard of them and heard that they were staying by the lake in the woods he took Henry and some of the younger children in the wagon to find them.

They tied the horses and wagon to a tree and walked into the woods that surrounded the lake. They found the family. They were fishing for dinner, had a small fire going and a small shelter neatly built of branches and boughs. Neither of the two children or the parents had shoes.

As Charlie and his children approached the father stepped towards Charlie and motioned his family to stand behind him. His fear, or concern, was very apparent to Charlie. Charlie understood the man's caution. He had no reason to trust Charlie. Charlie spoke "good day, I'm Charlie Mack. I come with my children to see how we can help." By that night the family was set up in Charlie and Clara's small shop behind the house. It wasn't much but it was dry, warm and a safe place for all. Charlie apologized for not having them stay in the house, it was full up with his own family and he felt the shop would give them privacy and more room. Thomas George and his family stayed in that shop until with Charlie's help they were able to build a small house of their own on their very own land. Right next to Charlie and Clara.

A friendship that lasted a lifetime was started with Charlie's welcoming words.

That first night, late into the morning hours after Charlie, Henry, Clara and the older children had helped the George's get settled Henry asked

Charlie "hows come you wanted to help when no one else would?" Charlie hesitated, he knew Henry would understand, but he did not like talking about it. Henry was a man now, a very young man, but he trusted him.

"Henry, I fought a war because I believed it was right to do so. No man has the right to own another man. How is that even possible? But that isn't enough. If one man has the ability to help another man, he ought to do so." Charlie did just that. He talked the owner of the mill into giving Thomas a job, vouching for him and his character. Charlie was a friend to Thomas and Thomas in turn was a friend to Charlie.

The town grew. The families grew and expanded. Charlie worked until the day they found him inside the mill, collapsed. Thomas picked him up and placed him on a bench. The doctor came and said he'd had a stroke. Thomas rode in the wagon with Charlie to his home and to Clara. They carried him inside where Clara and Thomas' wife Mabel nursed him. He would live but his right side was badly affected.

Thomas went to work every day and came home every night to eat a quick meal Mable would have ready for him. He would go to Charlie's house and get him out of bed and put him on his feet. He put the cane he had made in Charlie's left hand, pulled Charlie's right arm across his own shoulder and walk with Charlie. At first it was just inside. Then Charlie started pointing the cane and trying to speak, towards the door. They began walking outside for as long as Charlie could manage.

All the while they walked Thomas would talk. Telling Charlie the story of how they had met and he would never forget Charlie's first words "Good day I'm Charlie Mack". It became Thomas and Charlie's mantra for walking and talking. "I'm Charlie Mack, I'm Charlie Mack".

Charlie repeating those, and many other words that Thomas prompted from him.

The children would massage Charlie's right hand. They would curl his fingers and uncurl them. They would pull on his fingers while he tried to curl them. They would make him say the A, B, C's.

Henry had gone away to school but hurried home to be with Charlie when he received word of the stroke.

Within weeks Charlie wasn't using the cane. His hand still trembled some but he could use his fork and was practicing signing his name. His speech was coming along but it took great effort on his part. After a week of enjoying Henry being home he told him "you…go….school". Henry went back to school knowing Charlie was okay.

Charlie returned to work months later. His boss valued Charlie's knowledge, skills and ability to teach and motivate everyone. He only worked a few more years. When he left work for the last time many of the men standing behind him as he walked out shed a tear.

Charlie doted on Clara who doted on him. Thomas and Mabel were family, one door over. One day, though Thomas and Charlie would not live to see it, a great grandson of Thomas and Mabel would marry a great grand daughter of Clara and Charlie.

Charlie never stopped being the man he wanted to be for his family, his friends, his neighbors. When he died the grief was far spread. The funeral was large. The little cemetery he had chosen for his final resting place was far from town. Peaceful. And as in life, Clara beside him and Thomas and Mabel in the next plot. Charlie's stone read "I'm Charlie Mack". The strangers who would come to read the worn out letters decades and centuries later they would wonder what kind of name Im was.

Frank Martin

1899-1924

Opal Martin

1901-1930

"Opal! You are not one of the boys! Get in here!" Opal spun towards her mother and put her hands on her non-existent hips. "Don't you even think of sassin' me!"

Opal stomped her feet all the way to the house. Mother stood her ground. But only because her mother was standing within the house expecting her to 'correct' Opal and make her behave the way she thought Opal should behave. Mother wished she had Opal's spunk. "Why can't I play with the boys?!" She demanded of her mother as she stood toe to toe with her, even if she had to lean way back to see her Mother's face. For her tiny frame she held a mighty load of attitude. It nearly drove her mother to madness, and made her jealous of Opal. She wanted to be like Opal.

Opal's daddy loved Opal's attitude and brashness. Especially as he witnessed the effect his mother in law had on his wife.

"Boys play too rough Opal." Opal laughed and looked back at the group of boys waiting to see if she was getting in trouble. None of them was rougher then her. They teased her, and played as rough with her as they did with each other, but there wasn't a one of them who didn't admire her courage. And over the years most of them would come to adore her, some of them love her, but all of them liked her. Right at this moment they were all relieved it wasn't them getting in trouble.

"Opal you look a fright. Your grandmother wants you to make bread with her."

"I don't want to make bread. Why do I have to make bread and work while the boys all play?"

Opal threw her arm behind her to encompass all the boys, two of them her brothers.

Opal's mother agreed with Opal in theory. She struggled in her own way with the demands put on girls. Not that demands put upon boys were better. Just different. If her mother didn't live with them and voice her opinion 'round the clock it would be much easier. She could feel her own mother behind her in the house. She knew her ire was up at Opal's sass. She was torn between her own mother's demands and expectations and her daughter's frustration and unwillingness to conform to something she did not understand or agree with. She closed her eyes, wanting to run outside with Opal.

"Daddy!" Her eyes flew open at Opal's yell. Thank the Lord. Opal ran to him and jumped into his arms. Opal might be sassy but she was a good girl. And fair. The boys all smiled at Opal's daddy as he walked through the group of them. He plopped Opal down in front of her mother. He reached out and touched his wife's face. "Are we at yet another impasse?" He smiled. His wife tipped her eyes to her left and ever so slightly twitched her head. He knew immediately his mother in law was inside. He patted Opal's head "go play with those ruffians Opal". Opal spun with a shout and the children fled.

He took her hand and pulled her away from the house. Smiling at her, he knew how her mother got to her. The old woman had no bad intentions she was just solidly and irreversibly set in her ways. She wouldn't contradict him. He knew to make sure she heard him when he sent Opal to play.

"It's a beautiful day, yes?" She smiled at him, grateful. "Yes."

Opal and the boys played until everyone went their own ways to dinner. Opal's best friend Frank, two years older then her, walked back with her. "Will you be in trouble when you get home?"

Opal knew how things were with grandmother and mother. She felt bad for her mother, she would never have been able to defy her mother. Most of the time when Opal sassed she was directing it to grandma, but unfortunately mother was always the one standing between them. "No, daddy said I could play. It's okay." Of all the boys Frank was her favorite and he knew how strict grandma was. When they got in front of their houses neither slowed down they just split off from one another and hollered 'see ya' as they went towards their homes.

Though grandma made things harder, home was happy. Mother had the worst of it but even at that home was a good place. Grandma loved to bake and wished to teach Opal everything she knew. Opal would rather be chopping wood out back with her brothers. Grandma was a great seamstress and wanted to teach Opal how to make her own clothes. Opal would rather be whitewashing the house.

Opal couldn't always get out from grandma's reach and she did learn to bake and sew. Begrudgingly she did enjoy 'making' things but she never let grandma know or she would be tied to grandma and her ways all the time.

By the end of 1917 Frank had turned 18. He was drafted into the army. There was no doubt in anyone's mind that Frank and Opal would end up together. Frank asked Opal to wait for him. She told him "of course". Long before he left they talked about the war and what was going on in the world. It was frightening. Even if he had not been drafted Frank would have joined. Opal was angry that she couldn't join. She tried to join and hoped to be a nurse but she was too young and her parents would not sign for her to go. It didn't help that even when she was 16 years old she looked more like 12. Before Frank left she told him she was going to sneak away and lie about her age. Even she had to join his laughing when he told her no one would ever believe such a thing.

Opal did everything she could to help the war effort. She double planted the family's garden in the backyard. She participated in all of the county's war effort drives. She was ecstatic when one of daddy's friends who knew Opal asked daddy if she could work for him. In construction! He didn't have enough men to do the work. Daddy agreed. Mother was secretly thrilled for her. Grandma tutted.

Opal started working before Frank left. She started with cleaning up the job sight, keeping the tools in order, and being an extra set of hands and feet to run for things the men needed. All of the men were daddy's age or older. They all treated her well. In short time she was measuring, cutting and nailing framing for walls. The men all got a kick out of her not taking any gruff without giving it back. She was a fast learner and surprisingly strong for her small stature. The men enjoyed having her around and having someone to teach their skills to.

The day Frank left he put a bracelet on her wrist. "Write to me, as much as you can."

"I'll tell you all about where we are. Then we'll go back after the war." It was a horrific way to see the world but they often discussed the incredible things he would see.

Opal counted on that. Opal saved every penny she could, for her and Frank's future adventures. She and Frank wrote often but the war didn't always allow timely delivery. It wasn't until many weeks after Frank's family was notified he was seriously injured that Opal received a letter from him. He was in the hospital in England. He informed her in a shaky hand that he had lost his left leg and would understand if she no longer wanted to wait for him.

She replied quickly and to the point "I am waiting".

It was almost a year before Frank came home. On crutches, looking thin but healthy. Opal waited for him sitting on her parent's front porch. She waited until he came up on the porch. She waited until he reached his hand down and she took it. He said "you've waited long enough, lets get married".

They were married less than six months later. They moved into a small apartment owned by her employer. With the men returning from the war he had to let Opal go. But within days he hired her as a secretary/bookkeeper and he hired

Frank as a driver. The men at work adapted and outfitted the company's delivery truck with adaptive rods so Frank could drive using his hands and right leg.

Opal was still often requested on a job site. Her energy was unmatched. Frank still suffered from his injuries and woke up many nights sweating and rolling, sometimes screaming out. Opal would comfort him, holding him, reminding him he was home.

Frank would not or could not talk about the war. Not the horrors of it. But he spoke often and fondly of the men he served with and befriended. The men who he depended on and who counted on him. Opal loved the stories of these men. She loved how he spoke of them so much that she encouraged him to write his stories. Initially he balked at the idea. But during one of his frequent hospitalizations he took the notebook she offered him. And he wrote. He would always share what he had written with her. Opal grew to love the men her husband admired. They had conversations about them as if Opal knew them as well.

Opal noticed the stories did not include the war itself and she worried he didn't release the pain of it. She knew better then anyone how much he was affected by what he had seen, what he had done, what had happened to him and the other men who served. One day when he was home, unable to work, she brought him another notebook. "This one is for you Frank. Write the things you can't tell me. I won't read it. Unless you want me to." He took the notebook and sat it on the table next to his chair. He took her hand and pulled her on his lap. She knew this would not be comfortable for him but knew he would not want it to be this way.

"Opal I'm so sorry. I know this isn't what you waited for." So she could better look at him she shifted to sit on the arm of the chair and turned to him. Her hand playing in his hair. "You're everything I waited for. A kind man. A decent man. A loyal man. You're everything I look forward to."

"But all the things we imagined doing since we were kids…"

"It was about being with you, not the things."

Within a year Frank was gone. Died in his sleep between the time Opal got up to start their morning coffee and the time she returned to bring him a cup in bed.

Opal was well watched over by her family, Frank's family, and all the men at work. Her energy, that had been fueled by joy and love, was now fueled by love and grief.

Months after he died Opal discovered Frank's notebooks. The notebooks about the men he served with and met during the war were all stacked neatly on their bookshelf. But under his chair was a bundle of notebooks tied together with a ribbon. On the cover of the top notebook Frank had written "Opal, you can read this if you want, just know that all of the horrors I saw were released by your love. I thank you for helping me be set free. At least, as free as I could be."

Opal did read the notebooks. Several times. She herself began to wake up in the middle of the night in startled fits. She reread the stories he had written about his friends. Laughing and crying and sharing their carrying-ons through Frank's words.

She thought about how these men might appreciate these stories. She painstakingly typed the stories, then retyped them again to make them perfect. She had them printed into copies she could give to the men she could find. She did the same with the notebooks about the war, not expecting to give as many copies.

Over a year after Frank's death, with a promise from her boss that her job would be waiting for her when she returned, she left. She had contacted as many of the men Frank had written about, made plans, got train tickets and started her journey, that she could find. She carried the notebooks in one large suitcase, her clothes in a small valise.

She met the men, the soldiers. She recognized them in the stories as she got to know them. Most had wives or sisters with them when they would meet her. They would take her to lunch, or dinner, most often at their homes or their parent's homes. They carried her suitcases. Often times they offered to put her up. They all wanted to talk about Frank. They told her stories about him that she had not known. She knew her husband and wasn't surprised by the stories but deeply touched by how many lives he had touched.

She gifted each of them a copy of Frank's stories. Not a one of them took it without tears in their eyes.

Depending on how the meetings and conversations went Opal would give a copy of Frank's war stories. Of the 17 men Opal managed to meet in person she did not give the war stories to 6 of them.

She returned home after more then 4 months. Her travels having taken her across the country in a zigging-zagging pattern. She returned to her promised job, her savings nearly gone, and memories of her own adventures. In her heart the trip had been made with Frank. Just as they had talked about.

After she returned she received letters from the men she had met, some of the wives, sisters or parents. Their gratitude kept Frank's part in her life complete. Some of the wives expressed gratitude at better being able to understand what their husbands had gone through. Then letters from other men started arriving. Other men in the stories, or who had heard about the books Opal had made. Requests for the books arrived, some with money to cover the cost. If someone requested a copy and didn't have the money they received a copy anyway.

It became her passion to share Frank's words with the men he admired, the men who stood with him, made him laugh when laughing was unthinkable. To the men who held one another together as the world around them was torn and blown apart.

Many, many decades after Frank's death, grandchildren, great-grandchildren, and more, would come across Frank's words and see the old men they knew or had known, as a young man fighting a war that he did not create. A man in his prime.

When Opal died it was a shock and tremendous loss for everyone. Her funeral was attended by men and women who met her through Frank's words, her family, her grief stricken co-workers and boss. And a group of neighborhood boys grown up.

She was buried next to Frank in the little cemetery far outside of town.

Benjamin Butler

1837

Some say he was over one hundred years old when he died. But even those who were left behind when he died, have now been gone nearly two centuries. No one knows anything about him now. Just a name and a year.

Benjamin was special. Everyone knew it. He was born tiny. So tiny the only way to feed him was dip a cloth in milk and put it in his mouth. His mouth was so small he couldn't take his mother's breast. Each morning that they found him breathing was a surprise to them all. He was born long after his siblings. His next sibling was his sister Ella who was seventeen when he was born. Ella was put in charge of his care. Mama wasn't expecting a pregnancy. She didn't think she was able at her age, well into her fifties, to have a baby. She wasn't ignorant about child bearing. She just knew, or thought she knew, she was past it.

She loved little Benjamin but felt somewhat disconnected. Because she had only suspected a pregnancy a month before he was born she had not fully accepted it. Thinking it may have been something else bothering her stomach. He was born needing extra care and Ella was wonderful with him. Ella had a beau, Oliver. He came to be very fond of Benjamin. When they married shortly after Benjamin's birth he went with Ella to her new home with Oliver on his parent's farm.

Benjamin developed differently then other children. He didn't try to do anything. He just did everything. He didn't try to roll over, he just did. He didn't try to crawl, he just got up on his hands and knees and went. He didn't try to sit up, he just did it. One day he was sitting, he got into his crawling position, stood up and walked. Without so much as a wobble.

Benjamin watched his family. Everything they did, he mimicked. Except speak. He never spoke a word his entire life. He grew as tall as his brothers. But no matter how old he was there was a child-like quality to him. He was a joy to everyone. He learnt chores quickly. He could fell a tree, chop it up for firewood or saw it into planks for building something better then any of them. He worked the fields. He built things or tore them down. Whatever was needed. What seemed to make him happiest were the children and the animals. Child and animal alike went to him no matter where he was. He was most fond of Ella and Oliver's children. As a playmate to the first of their children, protector of the younger children.

Benjamin was never able to ask for anything but he gave everything he had to all of them. He never said a word against another human being. He gestured and acted with kindness and respect.

Benjamin never lived alone. But he lived joyfully everywhere he lived. He lived with Ella and Oliver until they passed. His grief was palpable. But when Ella and Oliver's daughter moved into the old homestead with her family and assured him everything would stay the same he appeared to adjust quickly.

And so it went. Benjamin continued taking care of the people who took care of him.

Benjamin never read a book, sang a hymn, or expressed great thoughts. But he lived greatly. When he died his family grieved. They buried him in the little cemetery out in the country. They could only put his year of death as no one alive was alive when he was born. No one knew his date of birth. They buried him and returned to a place that didn't feel quite right for a very long time. His silence was greatly missed.

Her Name Was Dottie

She lived in an old shack behind the butcher. It wasn't planned and the owner of the shack wasn't initially aware she was there. She had avoided everyone she could for a very long time. The short story is that the butcher let her stay in the shack after he found her hiding there and deduced she'd been there for some time. She had cleaned it, organized it and done no harm.

The longer story. When he went out to see if he could find some old knives he had thrown out there he walked in to find the shack clean and organized. Not as he had kept it all these years. As he looked over everything and found the knives he saw feet under the partial wall in the back of the shack. He yelled "come out! I see you!" He was a large man, and he was holding knives, he felt no fear. A small woman, dark brown, stepped out. He lowered the hand he had raised with his yell. She appeared terrified of him.   "What's your name?" He demanded roughly, more out of shock, then for any other reason.

"Dottie" she stuttered. He gestured around the room with his arm, she flinched and backed up. "Did you do this?" He realized he had waved the knives. He dropped them on the table where he had picked them up. She nodded her head.   He looked around and took in more of the shack. "Where'd you come from?"

"Georgia" she stuttered again.

"How did you get here?"

"Walked".

"Alone?"

"Yes."

"This is my shack."

"I'm sorry, I will leave." Though she stuttered she spoke well. The butcher looked around. He took in not only her orderliness but the cleanliness of what he had considered a place to just throw junk into.

"No. Stay." He wasn't sure what he was acting on but he knew from the looks of her she had nothing. "How long have you been here?" She shrugged. "Is that where you sleep?" He nodded at the partition she had been hiding behind. She nodded. He moved forward to go look. She flinched and covered herself with her arms. He backed up quickly. "I'm not going to hurt you". He stepped back towards the door. "I'll send my wife to check on you." He nodded at her. She returned his nod.

He went to leave and she said "knives". He picked the knives back up and left closing the door behind him.   He went right upstairs to where his wife was baking bread in their home above the shop.   He told her what had happened. She immediately started gathering items.   A quilt, some of her bread, some jam, and told her husband she would see what Dottie needed.

The butcher went back to work.   The butcher's wife went to Dottie.   They both had a general idea of what the woman had been through. Fortunately for Dottie she picked a shack to shelter in of people who believed in kindness and 'do unto others'.   She went to the shack and knocked on the door.   She could hear a sound like steps but so very soft.   She could see the girl, or woman, through a crack in the door.   She smiled at the eye looking through the crack and help up the items she had brought.

The butcher's wife and Dottie spoke for over an hour.   Dottie showed her the makeshift pallet she had been sleeping on.   Together they put the quilt on it. Dottie only had the clothes she was wearing. The clothing, like Dottie, was too thin. She had survived on foraging and fishing. She knew she only had herself to depend on.

Within a week the butcher had fixed the crack in the door of the shack and added a lock for her to feel more safe. He had looked for and fixed holes in the building and helped his wife bring in one of the old mattresses in their home that their children used to sleep on.

The butcher's wife had taken some dresses that no longer fit her to Dottie. They sewed them together, taking them in to fit Dottie. Dottie, in turn, helped the butcher clean his shop and he taught her how to wrap the cuts of meat.

Gradually he emptied the shack of all of the things he had been storing in there. Knocking on Dottie's door and asking if she could give him this or that. Until the shack housed only Dottie and her belongings. Dottie shared their outhouse with them but only after the butcher's wife convinced her that walking to the woods every day was not safe or necessary.

There were those in town as kind as the butcher and his wife. And there were those who were not. No one crossed the butcher or dared to be outright unkind to Dottie. Dottie was not comfortable around most people anyway. She preferred solitude and peace. She came to love and respect the butcher and his wife. She confided much to the butcher's wife. Dottie asked that she not share her story with anyone including, especially, the butcher. She made that promise to Dottie and only told her husband "we cannot be kind enough to her". The butcher knew his wife well enough to know that the tears in her eyes told more then she could tell him.

When the butcher's wife tried, once, to get Dottie to go on a visit with her to an elderly couple in need of prayer and a little help, Dottie balked. She did not like the process of meeting new people. She did not like leaving her very small but safe place in this world. She had never had that before. She did not want to step outside of the bubble of it. No one pushed her.

Dottie enjoyed the things the butcher taught her. But her most favorite thing was baking with his wife. She was a better baker then anyone the butcher's wife knew. Dottie soon took over the baking for the three of them, and for the baskets they made for the ill or the grieving.

Everyone in town came to love the good food. It got to the point where they thought some folks were faking illness just to get some of Dottie's bread or cookies.

It gave Dottie joy to know something she did was enjoyed.

The butcher and his wife agreed that Dottie should live in their home with them. But Dottie would not agree. She felt safe and protected in her little shack. They stopped calling it a shack and started calling it "Dottie's place."

The butcher and his wife, at Dottie's request, sat with her and had bible study every week. Dottie had the fundamentals of reading and the faith of a believer but she physically ached to learn more about her savior. The butcher and his wife enjoyed Dottie and all she brought to their lives.

Dottie was grateful for a place to call home, people she could trust, the safety being in their lives awarded her. Independence. Freedom. And the ability to quiet and fortify her soul.

It was many years after that first day when the butcher found her hiding in the shack that the butcher's wife, worried about Dottie not coming up the stairs, to join her for coffee, found her lying in her bed. She had laid down to sleep and never rose. Not in this life.

The butcher had his cousin build her casket and he and his wife took her to the old little cemetery. They were surprised to arrive and find dozens of towns people waiting. To say goodbye to Dottie. They had grown to appreciate her through the kindness she put into her baked good and her peaceful existence.

<u>Walter</u>

1821-1838

"Boy, hey boy, wake up!!"

The boy wanted to wake up. He struggled to open his eyes. One of the men lifted him "give him some water Joseph".

They managed to get the boy to swallow some water. But he wouldn't, or couldn't, wake up. Joseph and his brother Daniel got two long branches from the woods where they found the boy slumped against a tree. They fashioned a stretcher of sorts. All the while talking to each other and the boy. "We'll get him back to Ma. She'll take care of him."

"Come on boy. Wake up. You'll like Ma. She'll take good care of you."

"He's been through something Daniel, look at the bruises on him." They couldn't help but see the bruises. His clothing was torn, though what he wore would barely pass for rags.

They fashioned him as best they could to the stretcher. They covered him with the deerskins they'd been sleeping on. Fortune for this boy they were on their way home from scouting out some new land to farm. It took them a few hours but they got home and laid him down in front of the cabin to get Ma to come out. She heard them and came out to welcome them home and see what news they had.

She saw the boy and went to him, kneeling by him. She looked to her sons as she lay her hand on the boys cheek. The boy turned his head into her hand without opening his eyes. "We found him under a tree Ma. He hasn't woke up. Looks in pretty bad shape. He sipped some water but didn't wake."

Ma moved her hand around the boy's cheek and forehead. He was burning with fever. "Take him inside". She ran in and pulled the quilt back on her own bed. Joseph bent down and scooped up the boy, carrying him like a child to Ma's bed. Ma and the boys stripped him down and washed him. He had bruises on his body and his body was too thin to protect him from whatever had happened. Not an ounce of fat on him anywhere. Ma put poultices of moss and herbs where he looked swollen and cut. She kept rinsing a rag in cool water for his face.

The weather was almost warm during these early days of spring. But the nights were too cold to be out in with just what the boy had on. There was no way to tell how long he had been where the boys found him.

For two days Ma took care of the unconscious boy. Daniel and Joseph worked the farm, took care of the animals and put the word out to any of the folks nearby about the boy. Hoping someone knew something of him. No one did.

Ma spoon fed him water and broth. He was thin and broken. Was he beaten? Was he thrown from his horse? Ma watched over him like he was her own.

On the third day as she was giving him water and Joseph and Daniel were finishing up their venison stew the boy opened his eyes.

"Boys!" Ma whispered urgently. They came over and stood behind her. Looking at the boy looking at them. They saw fear.

Daniel spoke first. "Hey boy. My name is Daniel. This is my brother Joseph. This is our Ma. She's been taking real good care of you". The boy stared, his eyes darting back and forth between the three of them. Joseph told him "we found you under a tree in the woods. You're at our farm now."

Ma moved to lay her hand upon his cheek to check the fever. The boy flinched. Ma paused her hand but said "boy, no one here will hurt you, I promise you that." The boy closed his eyes as Ma laid her hand on his cheek. The boy, as he felt her gentleness turned his cheek ever so slowly into her hand. Just as he had done when he was unconscious. He couldn't tell them but it was the kindest touch he remembered. Ma started to move her hand away and as they watched a tear slid from under his eye. Ma wiped it away and put her hand back on his cheek.

"Boy". He opened his eyes to Daniel's voice. "Can you tell us your name?" The boy did not answer immediately. When he did it was barely a whisper. More like sound on breath. "Walter" was all he said. Ma told Daniel to get a cup with water. Joseph stepped in and propped up the boy's shoulders and head. Daniel gave the cup to Ma. Who put it to Walter's lips. Walter took a small sip then another. They laid him back down.

"How old are you?" Again it took time for him to answer. "Seventeen."

They let him rest for a few minutes. "Where are your people?" He opened his eyes and jolted. He looked around. "Franklin!" He called out. Ma and the boys looked at one another. "Who is Franklin?" Ma, took his hand. "Walter, who is Franklin?" A tear rolled out from under his eye lid.

Walter opened his eyes. He did not answer. He never spoke another word. He looked at Ma. If they could read his eyes they would know how much comfort he took from her, from all of them. How safe he felt. Finally.

He closed his eyes. He died later that day. Ma, Daniel and Joseph the only ones to grieve him.

Joseph's friend helped build a casket. They put him in old clothes of Daniel's, wrapped him in Ma's quilt that he had laid under his last three days of life. They buried him in the small cemetery. Joseph and Daniel made him a cross with "Walter" and the years that made him "seventeen". Ma put wildflowers under the cross.

Ma and the boys soon moved to land out west. She stopped at Walter's grave and put more flowers at his cross. Ma, Daniel and Joseph, the last to think of the boy Walter. Over the years the cross faded, fell, and was gone.

Walter remained, having died in a place he would have loved to have lived.

<u>John D. Baker, Jr.</u>

1871-1929

The last child born to Florence and John Sr. It made John Sr. happy to now have his boys out number his girls. Six boys and five girls. It was just about the last thing Florence did. She was wore out. She died when Junior, as they called him, was only five months old.

Senior put the girls in charge of raising Junior, along with everything else they did. Their burdens now increased not only caring for another child but adding their mother's work to theirs. Father was a strict task master. Not cruel, he didn't hit them, or deny them anything if he could make it happen. He just had expectations. He believed in work above all else. He was a very strong, tall, powerful man. Many judged him by this alone.

All the children worked. And they worked hard. Chores before and after school. Schooling was a must. In addition to their chores they had to sit nightly and go over their school work with father. In this way, father was educated. He had been denied any real education by his own father. He believed education was 'the way' to become better. It was only after each child became older that they realized they were actually teaching their father. None of them ever let on that they knew. And they did their best to help him.

Father did not know how to show emotion. He seemed curt, sometimes surly. But he was not uncaring. The children all knew this as well.

Junior's sisters did well by him. He was a kind child. Junior was too sensitive for Father's comfort. But Father tried to adjust. The boy grew up doing as he was asked and obeying his sisters. It wasn't until he went to school that he realized he was not like the others. His sisters suspected it but dare not voice it. Father and the brothers were too far removed from Junior's daily care to notice. If they did, they also did not voice it.

Like he did with all of his children he sat with Junior nightly to go over what Junior had learned during the day. This became the most time Senior spent paying direct attention to any of his children. Once this time began, it was appreciated by each in their own way. For the father and the child. Senior was still learning from the older children in school but he had now been educated well enough by the older children that he could help the younger children. None of them needed much help, they were all bright children. But Junior cherished the time with his father.

Once they began spending this dedicated time together, Senior and Junior grew close. The other children saw this and enjoyed the effect

Junior had on Senior. Senior appeared to soften. Though none of them would ever tell father this. While all of the other children focused on the facts of their education Junior brought home other lessons. Junior would tell Senior about the poetry the teacher would read. Geography lessons would be enriched by teacher telling stories of how other's lived. Teaching them about 'cultures'.

Senior soaked up the stories. He had a long denied curiosity. Junior fed his father's curiosity in a way the others could not. As he got older Junior would ask teacher about books and 'other worlds' (as he and father nicknamed other cultures). The things they had learned felt other worldly.

All of the children (especially the grown and older, some married) were nearly shocked when father agreed to go to a poetry reading at the school for the children. It was held in the evening so the parents could attend. Any child could read any poem. Junior was the only boy from his class who was reading. Father dressed in his nicest clothes, trimmed his beard and walked with Junior and some of the sisters to the school.

Father stood tall and proud as Junior read his own poem. He felt like everyone clapped the most for Junior. As father walked his children home he was surprised when out of the dark he could hear the word 'sissy' being hissed out towards him and his children. He knew it was meant for Junior. He stopped cold. Junior and his sisters looked at each other in fear. Father was angry. Something they seldom saw.

Father looked down at his children and spoke with his booming voice "children, no man is a sissy who shows courage before the ignorant, the uncouth and the cowards who hide in the dark".

His voice was like a controlled explosion into the dark. They could hear feet running away.

Father was not ignorant. When they approached home he sent the girls in. In a rare outwardly physical show of compassion he placed his hand on his son's shoulder. "Son, are there problems at school?" Junior looked at his feet. "No father." Father knew better. He knew more then his daughters or his sons ever thought he could. He patted Junior's shoulder. "You did well tonight." He chucked Junior under the chin. Junior looked up at him. "Do not judge yourself by ignorant men Junior." He nodded at Junior and pushed opened the door for Junior to go in ahead of him.

That night gave Junior something. Maybe it was confidence. Whatever it was it came from knowing his father would defend him. And that Father was proud of him.

Junior did not have an easy time in school. Academically he proved himself time and again. He did so well he intended to go to college. He wanted to study more. Maybe be a teacher. As he and his siblings all grew and moved on the most constant in all of their lives was their father. Though most of them were long out of school they loved sharing news and information with him. There was nothing he was not interested in. They began bringing him books and it wasn't long before he had a small library of his own. Though he did not know it himself, Father was a scholar.

In college Junior thrived. He found a small group of friends who accepted him and did not question about his lack of dating. They saw him as a fervent student who was focused on learning.

Junior would take the train home once a month or so. Always ready to regale Father with tales of academia. Often the house was hosting a grandchild or five. As he did with his own children Father sat nightly with any grandchild willing to share their day.

Junior graduated from college and returned home. No one in the family had moved far from home. They were a close, tight knit family. They depended on each other. Junior appreciated his father and felt valued in his family. As the town built a larger a school, a building that would house children's grade school through high school Junior saw opportunity. He applied for a teaching position and after several meetings with the school board he was surprised to be offered the position of Principal.

Senior was so proud of and impressed with Junior he actually took a day off work when the school held an open house for the community. He dressed up in his finest and went to every classroom. He sat in Junior's chair, in Junior's office, his arms outstretched with his large hands splayed out on Junior's desk. Surprising a few of his children and grandchildren when they walked in.

When Junior's oldest brother arrived he carried a wooden plaque. He handed it and a hammer and nail to Junior. Junior asked Father to move for a moment. He stood behind the chair and nailed the plaque right to the wall. When he moved they all read "Do Not Judge Yourself By Ignorant Men or Women".

Father looked at Junior, he remembered. He put his hand on Junior's shoulder. Then, to seal a special moment between father and son he chucked him under the chin.

Junior learned as he went. He had a good, logical sounding board in his Father. He remained in his father's home. Comfortable. And encouraged. Family never questioned him about why he didn't date. Or if he wanted to marry. Though they accepted him fully, knowing more than he thought they did, he never confided in them.

Junior created an atmosphere of acceptance and joy for learning at his school. He modeled his own teaching after the way he 'taught' his father. He had made his father feel like he was sharing, not that he knew more. In return, he encouraged Father to share his knowledge. He believed everyone had something worth sharing.

Father's library had grown considerably. He was able to obtain more stories through Junior's school library. He loved reading everything from children's stories to books written for women.

Junior dedicated his life to his school, his work, his family. No child went unnoticed. Every child was encouraged. Junior lived fully, happily, but for what he missed. He convinced himself the good he did, he achieved with sacrifice. There was no sadness in his heart. His life was good. Until that awful day when he was standing on the corner, down the street from the school. When the dairy truck's brakes went out. Junior was dead before the truck came to a stop by running into the building behind where Junior had been standing.

The family, the school, the community, flooded the school to pay their respects. The young boys who had taunted him, turned fathers and grandfathers to students of Junior's, came. Most of them regretting any cruelty they had shown to Junior.

When they took Junior to the old cemetery, the little cemetery barely held the throngs of people who came to say goodbye.

Father had the stone carved for Junior. "The bravest, kindest, most selfless man."

When the stone was set upon Junior's grave his oldest grandson drove Senior to the cemetery. He asked his grandson to give him a moment alone. He slowly made his way to Junior's grave. He laid his hand on the stone.

"Son, I'm sorry the world wasn't ready for you. Or always kind to you. I respected your right to privacy, but I sure wish I would have told you, I knew. I always knew. I hope you know, you were the best kind of man. Thank you for making me a better man." He patted the stone, wiped his tears, and left.

Sammy Downs

1899-1959

Grandson

"He's a heck of a worker". That's what everyone heard when they came into Old Joe's corner market. They would all stare out the window at the man across the street who Old Joe would be referencing. Dressed in dirty coveralls, the man was often outside of the factory where he worked as a janitor, and working on the factory vehicles. Old Joe would shake his head and keep ringing up the customer's orders. "Let me tell you, he's a gem of a fella". Old Joe had a soft spot for Sammy. He knew Sammy's story and felt protective of the man he had seen since he was born, when his grandpa would bring him in with him.

Old Joe had seen how the world treated Sammy. Ignoring him or making fun of him. Or dismissing him as not worth the effort to know.

He watched Sammy grow up amidst all of this. There had been a couple of boys who were kind to Sammy, watched out for him in school. They often all came in together after school for a candy or a pop. But when those two boys were drafted Sammy was left behind. One of those boys is buried in France. The other moved out west after the war.

Sammy lived with his grandpa. He was kind to Sammy, even when his parents were not. He loved his grandson, even when his parents did not. He stayed with his grandson, even when his parents abandoned him.

Sammy was different. In many ways. Physically he looked different but sometimes it took a few seconds of staring for people to figure out why. His face did not line up. It was as if the right side of his face was lower then the left side. His shoulders looked like a diagonal line had been drawn from the top of his left shoulder to the bottom of his right shoulder.

Sammy didn't talk much. He came into Old Joe's market every day for lunch once he started working at the factory. He would buy something to drink, a piece of fruit and whatever old Joe had on hand for him to eat. Old Joe and his wife started making him a sandwich every day out of the little deli in the store.

Every night Sammy went home to Grandpa. They had dinner that Grandpa had made. Sammy would clean up and do the dishes. Sammy kept the house outside maintained and clean, chopped the wood, whatever needed done. Grandpa kept the inside clean. Sammy would do anything for his Grandpa. And Grandpa would do anything for Sammy. They played cards together, went on long walks. They often took drives out through the country on the weekends when Sammy wasn't working. They took some long road trips. One to see the Grand Canyon and one to see the ocean, and many more just to see what they could find. They took turns driving the old truck they shared. Grandpa was great at fixing anything. Sammy was even better. They never had to worry about that old truck on their drives. Between them they could keep anything running.

Grandpa always told Sammy he was a genius. Grandpa knew Sammy, truthfully, was a genius.

They truly lived for one another. They enjoyed each other's company.

The older Sammy got the more his world appreciated him and respected his work and his abilities. Respecting his character topped all of it. When old Joe died, the letter Sammy wrote to his wife, she had it read at Old Joe's funeral. The compassion Sammy expressed made her feel like he knew Old Joe as well as she did. His words felt like he had pulled them from her heart.

The factory where Sammy worked wanted him to move up. To supervise maintenance, and maintain all of their equipment and vehicles. Sammy would do anything they asked of him, except supervise others. He knew he could do anything with machines and tools. He knew his limitations with people. The factory accepted this, not wanting to lose him.

Every time he shared work stories with Grandpa, Grandpa sat up straighter with pride as they ate their dinner. In turn, it filled Sammy with joy to see his Grandpa's pride in him.

The morning Grandpa got up and Sammy wasn't already making the coffee-he knew-before he found Sammy. He walked into Sammy's bedroom and found him lying in bed. Peaceful like no one on earth ever is. He knelt by

Sammy's bed, took Sammy's hand, and prayed for his grandson.

He seldom ever used the telephone but he called his neighbors. The husband and wife rushed over. They made calls. They got the old cardboard box off of the shelf in the closet. The one that Grandpa and Sammy had put their papers in if one of them ever needed it. All of the instructions for their living without the other one. They stayed with him until Sammy was taken away, helping straighten Sammy's room, making arrangements with Grandpa and making sure he had something for dinner.

The box was still lying on the kitchen table when the neighbors came back the next morning and found Grandpa sitting in his chair. He had joined Sammy in a peaceful place. They believed Grandpa had only hung on as long as he did to be with Sammy so Sammy was never alone.

They used the information in the box to help get Grandpa and Sammy laid to rest next to one another. Buried in a little cemetery they had never heard of.

They came out to the cemetery after the stone mason let them know the stones had been set. Next to Sammy's stone was his Grandpa's stone:

Samuel Downs

1869-1959

Grandpa

Cassandra Lanier

1903-1968

Cassie moved to town when she was in her twenties. As she gradually got to know folks, they learned about her. She had no siblings. Her parents both died when she was in her teens. She shared very little of her past.

Cassie rented a small apartment behind a diner. It wasn't long before she was working at the diner and at the small local hospital in the house keeping department. She was kind and friendly to everyone. If she ever judged anyone no one ever saw it. She was a hard worker and appeared to live frugally. She walked everywhere until she had been in town for about five years and bought herself an old Model T. She loved that car.

On her rare days off you would see her with no top on the car, a scarf on her head, heading out of town to explore. These were the only times

Cassie was really alone. Work filled her mornings, days and evenings. She enjoyed people. But her drives were for her.

Cassie was a larger than average woman, not petite, not exactly pretty. But there was something so appealing about her. She was adored. Cassie had many opportunities for dates and suitors. But she kindly declined all. She would tell her friends, without any details, how badly a young relationship had gone and she felt happier and safer alone.

Cassie was 'seen' by her employers at the hospital. They saw her dedication and her skills working with people. Many were the times supervisors tried to talk her into becoming a nurse. They saw how compassionate she was, and even as a housekeeper, she demonstrated a natural skill with people. Often she helped outside of her duties. Cassie always thanked them for the encouragement but never pursued it. She said she was happy doing what she was doing. She felt she was able to help others, including her co-workers, by being her best at her job. After many years she did accept an offer to be supervisor of her department. She developed her own training program. Many components of it were adopted by other divisions in the hospital to include in their training. No one was surprised when staff under her tutelage did end up becoming nurses. Cassie attended every single graduation/ceremony of any of her staff becoming nurses. There were more than a few graduations of doctors, and one who became an attorney.

In truth Cassie celebrated all of her friends accomplishments. And grieved in their losses. She lived joyfully whether around others or alone. Though she didn't need to she still opened the cafe in the mornings because of convenience and she enjoyed the camaraderie.

Cassie's life was extraordinary in a very ordinary way.

The morning the regulars showed up at the diner for their coffee and eggs and found the door locked they knew something was wrong. When there was no answer at her door and her car, not the Model T but her upgrade to a Chevy Belair, was still parked they called the landlord/diner owner.

They found Cassie on the floor of her bedroom. She was taken to the hospital where groups of people gathered. Cassie never regained consciousness. The charge nurse was one of 'Cassie's Nurses'. She took care of Cassie herself. She discovered Cassie's secret. She sent everyone away. She spoke with the doctor, a friend of Cassie's. No one but the nurse, the doctor and the coroner ever knew that Cassie had been born a man.

Her friends had often been to her home. For dinners, to pick her up, for counsel, or just for drinks and laughs. They knew her love of detail and orderliness. They easily found her will and were not surprised at finding it with detailed information. They were a little surprised at still no information about her life before coming to town being any where in her meticulous files. They were all surprised at her having amassed a fortune of almost $400,000. But then they went back to not being surprised at her charity of that fortune going to scholarships and service organizations.

Her small tombstone had already been paid for. Her staff, coworkers and friends had a bronze plaque with her image, her years of service, and a quote:

"Live with kindness
Give with love,
Be both."

In hangs in the hospital to this day.

<u>Albert Booker</u>

1904-1971

He sat quietly in his backyard. The fenced in, trees growing higher than the fence, bushes growing almost as high as the fence, backyard.

Completely closed in. He had spent years planting and letting everything around the perimeter of the yard grow. But within that perimeter everything was manicured. Flowers growing, stunningly, within pots and planters, in the ground. Every where.

The only entrance to the yard, the back door from the house. The house, sparse and tidy. Plain. It was a contrast to the life and joy of the colors in the backyard.

As the stars came out and the yard darkened, he stood. Gratefully he surveyed the beauty. He never tired of it. Not ever. It was Thursday night. The prearranged time to call the kids. They took turns, alternating weeks. Long distance was expensive. They spoke long enough to check in. He could get the quick updates on the grandkids, the kids and their jobs and spouses. Each of the kids would be encouraged and relieved to talk with him and hear he was doing well. They worried about him.

Albert couldn't face the embarrassment of divorce. He moved after all of his children were grown and on their own. His little cottage, in the little town, gave him great comfort. It was a 4 hour drive from what had been home. Far enough away to give him peace. Close enough that if he had to get back for something one of his kids needed he could do so relatively quickly. He learned quickly that he enjoyed solitude. He enjoyed people through work and through some social events with neighbors. But his time learning about planting and cultivating his own piece of calm, small as it was, fulfilled him.

The children and grandchildren would visit. Each time they would be newly impressed with his home and his garden-yard. They would leave feeling good about his world. Then they would return to their homes and worry would set in a-new. Again. Until their next visit.

Albert sat easily in this space. Here he could contemplate his purpose. His good deeds and his failures. He liked the process of evaluation and summation. He read the news. He read books. Where others, perhaps, thought he only existed, Albert felt he thrived. He planted himself within everything he sowed and felt himself grow. He felt peace like he had never understood it before. And to those who knew him, he exuded peace.

Seldom did he go visit the children if he wasn't called upon to do so. He loved them and the 'grands' completely. But driving back was like driving into a shadow. It was a little darker, a little sullen, a lot uncomfortable. After he was diagnosed he made the drive. They planned a big dinner together, he and his children and grands. After dinner when the grands were all playing or otherwise occupied - he told them.

When he drove back home he knew it was the last time he had to make that drive. The children tried to talk him into coming back and staying with them. After one attempt, by one of his sons, to talk him into coming back on a phone call the son's wife interceded. She took the phone from her husband and assured Albert she would take care of it and call him back. After hanging up, to her husband she said "he is happy and at peace. Let him enjoy his garden for as long as he can. You're making him hurt by asking him to do something for you. Instead of you doing this for him." He called his father. Apologized. And did, with his siblings and families, all that they could for him.

When Albert died he was in the hospital for only two days. With all of them there. Before the graveside service all of Albert's children went to Albert's garden. They cut all of the flowers and took them with them to the old cemetery. Once interred they covered the grave with mounds of flowers.

To this day random flowers pop up on one grave. It's a lovely scene.

<u>Natalie Simms</u>

1881-1959

"Why you gotta be so mean lady!" The little boy, Ned, wailed at 'Old Lady Simms' as he rubbed his ear where she had pinched him.

"Why do you have to keep trampling my vegetables? I need my vegetables!" She wasn't lying or exaggerating. But Ned was right too. She was mean.

His new puppy had gotten loose and Ned chased the puppy to Old Lady Simms' garden. Not seeing her crouched in the tomatoes carefully picking the ripe tomatoes and pulling weeds. If she was lucky she could sell some for a little extra money.

Being an elderly widow with no family or friends she lived a lonely existence. Ned had heard plenty of folks say it was her own fault. Ned had always felt sorry for her. But she'd never pinched him before either. He has family and friends. Even at 7 years old he knew how bad he would feel without them. He'd probably be mean too. But not the kind of mean to pinch little kids.

"I wasn't trampling them! My puppy came running in here and I tried to get 'im". He had just stood up from catching the puppy when he looked up and saw her just as she grabbed his ear.

"You need to be better about caring for your things. Maybe you ought not have a puppy if you can't care for him."

By now Ned was crying. "My ma and pa say I'm very good and re-re-responsible! Maybe that's why you don't have friends. Cause you aren't good at taking care of them!" He yelled it so fast that he surprised himself. Even more than Natalie, who was shocked at Ned's outburst.

Before she could reply he turned and ran. He ran until she could no longer see him.

Slowly she gathered her things. She was sore from working so long, and on the ground. She didn't mean to pinch him so hard. She went inside and washed the tomatoes. Maybe she better just can them. After everyone hears about her pinching Ned they wouldn't buy tomatoes from her anyway. She sighed as she tried to think of even more ways to pinch her pennies.

After cleaning the tomatoes she made herself a tomato and butter sandwich with the last of her homemade bread. She sighed softly again. She was so tired. She decided to wait until tomorrow and can some tomatoes and bake bread.

As she had done since her husband Lowell had died over twenty years ago she sat at her little table by the window that overlooked her street and wrote to him in her composition book. She lay the pen down on the open book when she was done. She was so overcome with exhaustion she decided to lay on the bed. If she was lucky, she thought, she would sleep until tomorrow.

Tomorrow, on earth, didn't come for Natalie. It was many days before anyone found her. And it was only because little Ned went by her house several times for those days-hoping to see her so he could whisper "I'm sorry". He knew he didn't have the nerve to approach her. But he kept seeing her sad face, when he yelled at her, in his dreams.

When he told his parents what had happened and how he hadn't seen her out, they left him home, went to her house, but she didn't answer their knocks. They contacted the sheriff. He found her right where she had laid down, so weary.

It was thirty years after her death when he was cleaning out his parent's home after their deaths. Pa first, then Ma. That Ned found a stack of carefully wrapped composition books. They were very old. He started reading and was surprised to discover Natalie Simms story. Old Lady Simms life in his hands. It took him three days to finish all of the notebooks. Each entry started with "Dear Lowell".

Ned discovered in her reflections the things she dreamed of as a child, a young bride. The importance Lowell was to her and how she grieved for him until the day she died. Her entries were as if she was having conversations about her day, or about her memories. Stories of her own childhood made him laugh and made him nostalgic for his own. He came to know her husband through her remembrances. He learned about his little home town and laughed at many of the things she wrote of because she was so on point with her observations. But some things made him sorrowful for her. There was no bitterness in her memories, only in the 'current' time of her writing. He was sad when he started reading the last notebook. He enjoyed the reading as much as any book he had read. When he turned to the last page with written words he was suddenly reliving her last day. This time from her perspective.

She wrote how she had woken to a sunny day and it made her miss her husband. What should be a beautiful day was just more lonely-knowing-it would be lonely. There would be no family or friends coming to pay a visit or check on her. She was too tired to work in the garden but knew she must. She wrote, sadly-not angrily, about 'that little Ned'. She not only shocked herself at what she had done but she was horrified at what she had done. Even more horrified at how this little boy saw her. When she saw his face she knew what she had become. Her last lines - "I sit here sobbing at what I have become. I hope to see that little boy to tell him how sorry I am. I am so sorry Ned."

Ned ran his hand over the page. Her hand was likely the last to touch it. It took him two weeks to find where she was buried. He was disheartened to see neither she, nor her husband who was buried two plots away from her, had headstones. He ordered and paid for her headstone, and for Lowell's. On hers he had a tomato engraved and 'wife of Lowell Simms'. He made sure she and her husband were connected. On Lowell's he had 'husband of Natalie Simms" engraved.

When the monument company let him know the stones had been set he went out to her grave. He placed a tomato on the ground in front of her stone and whispered "I'm sorry".

Nelson Grant

1920-1943

As did over 100,000 other United States citizens, Nelson enlisted in the army within days of Pearl Harbor being attacked. He told his foreman on his way out the door of the factory. The man shook Nelson's hand and wished for the good Lord to watch over him.

At dinner that night he waited until after grace was said. He was certain what he was doing was the right thing. Mom and dad always told him to do the right thing.

While mom, dad, sister Loreena and brother Phillip were filling their plates he cleared his throat. Mom looked at him expectantly. Dad held his plate mid-air. Lorena kept filling her plate but he saw she immediately started to tear up. Phillip hadn't even heard him. "I enlisted today".

Dad put down his plate. Mom bowed her head. Loreena, even at 12 years of age, knew what 'enlisted' meant. She looked at mom and dad to gauge their reactions to see how she should react. Phillip said "I wish I could". Dad stood up. Snapped into attention and saluted Nelson. In turn he jumped up and returned the salute to his father. A veteran of World War I. Dad came around the table and hugged him. Mom, stood up and joined him, then came Loreena and Phillip.

They all sat down. No one moving. Until dad started eating the mashed potatoes he had managed to get on his plate before the announcement. Slowly everyone resumed eating.

That night, in the room they shared, both Phillip and Nelson lay awake in their beds. Phillip asked softly "are you scared?"
Nelson, just as softly, said "yes".

Phillip replied "yeah".

The hardest thing to do upon waking was going
to talk to Betty. His high-school sweetheart. His
life long friend. They had known each other all
their lives. Nelson and Betty knew each other
through and through. She knew he was going to
enlist but she had been at her grandparents farm
the last few days helping out since grandma had
twisted her ankle. He walked to her house. She
opened the door and came out on the porch.
Without saying a word he took her hand and
started walking. He walked with her to the
school they had both attended and graduated
from together. He went in the open doors to
the-all-familiar building and walked to the
cafeteria/gym. Where, in their junior year,
having been friends forever, he kissed her for the
first time. Not knowing until that minute the
power of his feelings.

People, students and teachers were in the school. The only person in the gym when they went in was the janitor. He was pushing a gigantic dust mop up and down the length of the floor. When he saw Nelson drop to one knee he quickly and quietly left the gym to give them privacy.

"Betty. I don't have any fancy words. But I have all the love any man could have for a woman. Will you marry me?" Betty reached down with both hands, took his face between her hands and said "yes".

Within days they were married. They spent their honeymoon night one town over at the small inn. They returned home in time for him to spend a day with family and friends. Saying goodbye. Being prayed over. Hugged so much he had bruises on him.

He left by train for boot camp. It was during a physical examination after weeks of daily training and humping that Nelson was ordered to step out of line and go with the private attending the doctors.   The bruising on Nelson's torso concerned the doctors. Nelson was ordered to the barracks, no training, until further testing could be completed.

It was a somber day when Betty picked up Nelson at the same train station. He didn't want to see anyone but her.   They went to her grandparent's farm where they set up house in what used to be the farm hand's bunk house. Grandpa had done everything he could to make it comfortable for them.   For two days they stayed huddled in their little home before going out to be with other family.

Nelson was embarrassed to be coming home. While others were going to war he was going home because of something called leukemia. Something in his blood, something wrong with his blood.   He didn't understand it all until several trips to the hospital and appointments with doctors. He and Betty asked question after question. They thought if they knew more they could do more. He had blood transfusions that seemed to make him feel better. Or so he thought. But always the tests, the bruising, and the same response from the doctors. It was not better. It was not cured.

Nelson lived long enough to see his son Kenneth born. He did not fear death itself. But he struggled knowing he wouldn't be here to teach his son how to play, how to work, how to grow into being a man. He spoke with his parents and Loreena and Phillip about all of the things he wanted his son to learn from them, as he had. And he thanked them for being the family that they were.

Nelson held Betty and Kenneth as often and as long as he could. He breathed in their aromas. He hoped to leave the feeling of his embrace imprinted in their memories. Upon their very being.

Nelson and Betty lived as joyously as they could. Not all days were good. Not all days were bad. Smiles were found even on the bad days. The old farm hand bunk turned home was full of love. Nelson was the first person Kenneth walked to. Nelson was the only man Betty would love. Nelson knew his life was precious and he would live on in both of them.

Any friends leaving or returning from war came to see Nelson and salute him. Betty had made sure they all knew his self imposed shame at not being able serve his country. Nelson's nightly prayers included prayers for the soldiers he knew, and the soldiers he didn't.

When he died his father covered his casket with the flag. Any friends who were home and had a service uniform wore it to his funeral.

Betty and Kenneth continued to live on her grandparent's farm. Just a few miles from the cemetery where Nelson was laid to rest.

When Kenneth served in Vietnam he carried his father's picture in his book of psalms. The book and the picture took up residence in his breast pocket for the entirety of his service. When he returned home he gave both to his mother. It was the only way Kenneth could think of to honor his father's desire to serve his country.

Unmarked

He ran through the night. He and Walter had gotten separated as they ran through the fields and woods. Too scared to stop. Too scared to holler to one another. They ran further away from one another when all they wanted was to run together.

Franklin adored his big brother Walter. When they decided to run, each knew they would not go without the other. They had nothing so they could take nothing.

Franklin lived, terrified. He was almost used to it. But Walter had always been there. Even through the worst of it. Now he ran alone and knew a terror he had never known before. He ate berries if he could find them but it was past season for many to be hanging on. He drank from creeks. He slept under trees, and a couple of times in trees.

He was tired all the time. His already neglected and abused body was not prepared for this additional punishment. He was hot during the day and he shivered in the cold nights. He tried to build a fire but then fear of it showing where he was made him stamp it out. He tried to stay warm within a bed of pine needles.

Franklin was alone like he had never been. He wanted to be with Walter. That's all he thought of.

One day he could run no more. He sat, in the sun, feeling its rays finally bring him some warmth and chase the cold out of his bones. He lay back in the grass. His bruised and too thin body barely clothed. He closed his eyes and saw Walter. They ran to one another. Laughing. Hugging. Safe.

A group of hunters found him. Days too late. They could tell the child had been abused.

Bruises still evident. All of them fathers. All of them disturbed by the little body. They wrapped him in a blanket and buried him in an unmarked grave in the little cemetery nearby. Standing over his grave they prayed solemnly for his soul. Over the years those men would often tell of the young boy's body they found and buried. Hoping someone would know who he was. No one ever did.

Franklin would never know he was buried within 50 feet of the only person he needed in his life. His brother Walter.

Colt Greenbriar

1900-1951

They should have put 'Poor Old Colt' on his headstone. It was probably said more often about him when referencing him than any other moniker.

Colt was an only child to Elizabeth and Harold Greenbriar. Though they provided well for Colt they also set him up for a life time of misery. They instilled, or rather burdened, him with the responsibility and an obligation to them. They expected Colt to put them before all else. Before his schoolwork or play as a child. Before his needs as a young teen and developing adult. The grief and guilt bestowed on him before the handful of dates he managed to go on wasn't worth the anticipation of their lamenting and shaming him upon his return.

He didn't go to his high school graduation because dad was going to get his grass cut even if it did give him a heart attack. The manipulation they used on him was so transparent but he didn't feel like fighting it. By then Colt was resigned to his misery. He shoved his cap and gown in his closet and spent his graduation day cutting the grass and every other chore that took away any fun or accolades he would have had. He was accustomed to nothing being about him. Many of his friends and neighbors saw him cutting the grass when he should have been at his graduation. Fortunately his friends knew nothing would be done for him, they snuck to his house that night, made him join them by climbing out of his bedroom window and they had their own celebration just for him.

Colt would miss school. It was his only socialization. He was well liked. He enjoyed learning. It was his getaway time.

He needn't have worried.

He went right to work at the hardware store. It turned out to be the best part of his life. Work became his getaway. Home was his job. It's not that he worked all the time at home. It was the expectation of his parents for him to be there, always.

It was the hardware store where Colt had a life, friends, experiences. Over the years the owners became his friends, his family. They had birthday parties for him. Celebrated holidays with him. Customers became friends. His time there was full of joy. And work. He learned as he went and was very good at what he did. Through the owners, the contractors and regular folks fixing things on their own he became efficient at electrical, plumbing and building. His boss often encouraged him to go to school. He felt Colt would make a great engineer, architect or contractor.

Colt loved the idea. But he knew he couldn't. As frustrating as his parents were they had become so dependent on him he knew they wouldn't make it without him. As much as he was willing to do for his parents, which was a lot, he still had moments when he wanted to bolt. Run as far as he could. He dreamed of going to school or moving on into other fields of work. Everyone both admired him and pitied him. Some felt it was his decision so it was on him if he was unhappy.

But most everyone just liked him. He had fixed up the furthest back room in the old, very large and long building of the hardware store. He put some chairs around an old rug. He could take breaks, come in early or stay late. It was a place where he didn't have to deal with expectations.

Sometimes he would look around and imagine a place of his own. And sigh. Someone put a radio in the room. Someone else put in a table. It was a break room for everyone.

The hardware store was central to any relationship Colt had. The other shops and businesses on the street were like his neighbors. His life had comfort and joy. It was just backwards to how others lived.

The day after he turned 32, after a long day at 'work' Colt took his time walking home. How many times had he contemplated his parents, his life and how he handled his decisions, on this walk. Though his parents expected everything from him he knew he could leave at any time. Or not give into their demands. But he couldn't, or chose not to. When he was younger he would dream of ways to confront them. Or leave them. As he got older he just felt sorry for them. Others may pit him but he pitied his parents.

As he walked up to the door of the small house something wasn't right. The house was dark. It was too still. Just before he started to grab the door knob to open the door he smelled gas. He had to step back when the odor hit him hard in the face as he opened the door.

He took his shirt off and covered his face. He ran in the house trying to find his parents. It was dark but he feared turning a light on. He checked their bedroom and living room, throwing open the windows as he went. He had to run outside. He was dizzy and gagging. He ran around to the back door and went down the hallway to the kitchen. He turned around when he saw them and walked back out leaving the door open behind him. He made it outside before he started retching.

He nearly passed out. One of the neighbors saw him and yelled for her husband. They ran to him.

The funeral for both of his parents was a large affair. Most who attended were there for Colt. He hadn't slept well, closing his eyes brought the vision of his parents into full view. He couldn't unsee it. Eating made him retch again. Sipping water was all he could handle for two or three days.

Once his parents had been removed and they could go into the house they discovered what had happened. The gas line to the stove had cracked in half. From the coffee cups on the table and his mother still in her nightgown Colt knew they must have been there since morning.

Cold never spent another night in the house. His parents were buried in the cemetery of the small church they attended. He stayed in the little room at the hardware store until he got an apartment above the bakery. He sold the house. Moved into his apartment. And was grateful for his community.

Such conflicting emotions he dealt with. Grief and sorrow at what life had done to his parents and how death took them. And yet a feeling of freedom, of being able to breathe freely. It was sometimes difficult to process. He carried guilt for feeling free after his parent's tragic deaths. But he couldn't deny it.

The 'poor old Colt' sentiment intensified after his parent's deaths. But like his own feelings, others felt bad for having feelings of hope for Colt.

Slowly life took on a normalcy for him. It took him months to realize, and act on, not having to go home. There was no expectation. He could do what he wanted, when he wanted. It was a harder adjustment then anyone knew or would understand.

He started dating Caroline when he was 35. They married before he was 38. Caroline made him laugh. They loved to get in their car and drive for hours. They took great pleasure in back country roads and old barns. They even bought a camera and started taking pictures of barns that they both found odd, or stunning or full of character.

After his first heart attack at 47 he told Caroline his wishes if he were to die. When he died at 51 she had him buried in the furthest away cemetery that they had come across during their drives. A little cemetery in the country. All of his friends who went to the funeral assumed it was to be far from his parents.

Margaret O'Malley
1822-1922

I saw a lot. Too much, I sometimes think. I lived through wars, and peace, poverty and wealth. My homes have been rough hewn cabins with dirt floors to homes considered luxurious by many standards. The fiscal standing at any point in my life was not an indicator of the level of happiness or contentment of my life.

My dirt floor home that housed my parents and siblings and myself was one of the happiest of homes. We worked hard for everything we needed. We had little in the way of possessions unless it was something we could make. But we had everything in the ways of comfort. We had strong, loving arms that held us and protected us. Strong minds that showed us how to make-do or make better. Strong principals that formed us and guided us our entire lives.

While the cabin was rough and life was hard work it was also full of joy and glory. Never was work so hard that we couldn't pick wild flowers, or watch an eagle soar, or sit under a starry night and listen to stories of our parent's childhood and of their own mischievous antics. Laughter was part of our foundation.

The hard work of our youth prepared us for lean times. When others fretted on how to get by, we knew how to feed ourselves, and others. Most times hard work would see us through any tough times.

We knew little, precious little, from schooling. But we could all read, write and do math. Reading was something I found sacred. Until each of them died, my siblings and I wrote letters to one another and gifted books to one another when we could. We valued learning.

I had bad things happen to me. Some truly unpleasant things. But none of these things lessened the value of my life or who I was. The worst of things in my life were done to me, and those things didn't say anything about who I was. The only things that lessened my value, in my opinion, are the things that I'm ashamed of. The things that I've done that I knew better than to do. But did them anyway.

From the dirt floor cabin I grew. I married and moved into a cabin with a floor and a husband. My husband was killed during the civil war. We were never blessed with children. I carried sorrow and grief, as many did, like a pack on my back. It was heavy. But I shouldered it. After several years I married a widower who's children had all grown.

I was lucky. Both of my husbands were kind men. Good men. Hard working men.

My life was long. Honestly, sometimes it was quite boring in the living of it. That's not to say it wasn't full of busy work because it was. But there were times in life that felt mundane. These mundane times, though, were a blessing. They high-lighted the times I may have otherwise taken for granted. Who would, nowadays, be excited about indoor plumbing, or electricity or the telephone? Living without these things sure made the getting of them all the more special. I have to be honest though. There were times after the getting of them that I wish they had never been invented. Believe it or not it took some getting used to having a toilet in the house.

I would say the same thing about the automobile. I prefer a horse. And a buggy or wagon. Those automobiles are too big, too powerful and too smelly.

I could tell stories about my life. The changes I've seen. The changes I wish I hadn't seen. But

I really just want to thank the good Lord for giving me this life. I feel like my time here was a lesson. I learned much. Probably more than I realize.

One lesson was about appreciation. Looking at a parent, or sibling, or husband or friend and knowing my life was made better because they were with me. I am so thankful I had the good sense to let people know what they meant to me while I still could. I lost so many along the way. And not one loss burdened me with "I wish I had told them what they meant to me". Because I always did.

Another lesson is that 'here' isn't forever. And we all need to be grateful about that. One hundred years was granted to me. I thing it was a-plenty long enough. This life here wears you down for a reason. We ain't meant for eternity here. It's just one of our stops.

I'm gone now. My body laid to rest, as they say, but really just deposited because it isn't needed any more, in a little cemetery that's nearly forgotten. And that's okay. All who passed through here, like me, matter. Our stories live on in the energy that moved on from here. Even if here, we are barely remembered.

Whether the world at large knows my story, or not, doesn't matter. We all go the way of dust. We enter. We exit. We were here. Now we're somewhere else.

Lesson lived. On to the next one.

More books by C Faherty Brown at:

lulu . com